T0148413

GUNFIGHT AT DUTCHMAN'S WELL

By: Dr. Carl R. Stekelenburg

2011

Order this book online at www.trafford.com
or email orders@trafford.com

Most Trafford titles are also available at major online book retailers.

Printed in the United States of America.

ISBN: 978-1-4269-7271-3 (sc)
ISBN: 978-1-4269-7273-7 (e)

Trafford rev. 07/11/2011

www.trafford.com

North America & International
toll-free: 1 888 232 4444 (USA & Canada)
phone: 250 383 6864 • fax: 812 355 4082

DISCLAIMER

This is a work of fiction. No persons or events are true or actual. While historical characters may appear, any resemblance to a person living or dead is purely coincidential and a product of the author's imagination.

ABOUT THE AUTHOR

Dr. Carl R. Stekelenburg is a single man, blinded in 1993 in a mistaken identity attack. He was reared in the Midwest having lived in Minnesota, Iowa, Missouri, Oklahoma and Texas. Following graduation from college in Oklahoma, he served in the United States Air Force stateside during the Vietnam War. After his military service, he was an educator and administrator in Florida and Georgia. Upon completion of his doctorate in education at the University of Georgia in 1991, he was hired as Superintendent of Schools in Folkston, Georgia where he was attacked and clubbed blind in 1993. He is the father of two daughters, Tammy and Jenny.

Dr. Stekelenburg is the author of three previous books, **"The Burton Murder and Other Short Stories", "Blind Date"** and **High Plains Cowboy".**

He now resides in LaGrange, Georgia. After eighteen years of blindness, he continues to enjoy books on tape from the Library of Congress and authoring novels.

"Blind Date" tells the true story of how he was blinded in 1993.

PROLOGUE

Some men in the United States traveled out west in search of land, gold, silver, furs and adventure, or to escape the Civil War raging in the Eastern United States. Many of them were unaccompanied by women. As a result, a business developed in mail order brides. In Santa Fe, New Mexico Territory, the local mail order bride business placed ads in European newspapers. One such ad appeared in the Rotterdam Gazette and was read by three sisters. One of these girls, Louise, had been previously married to Sid Burt. Louise and her unmarried sisters all responded to the ad. Each received several replies. Their mother Julia was concerned that they would be traveling alone to America, so Julia Roosma asked her nephew, Jon Roosma to escort them to America, where they managed to meet their mail order companions.

Events in New Mexico lead to the gunfight at Dutchman's Well.

During this adventures, Jon Roosma traveled to Fort Worth, Texas where he met a Cherokee Princess.

Chapter One begins his story!

CHAPTER ONE

Jon was riding his gelding on the North Sea dike in Holland, also known as The Netherlands. He was sitting astride his buckskin gelding under a 100-year-old oak tree in the shade, when a young boy approached Jon with a note from Jon's Aunt Julia. The lad handed the note up to Jon and then fell in the grass laughing, while he stuck his hand in the grass and shouted, "I'm holding back the sea." Jon answered, "That's an old wives tale. This dike has been here for over 500 years, at least. See those sheep and cattle grazing? I'm herding them for the people of Rotterdam. Your finger's not going to hold back the North Sea, child." They both laughed at the thought. Jon said, "Let me jot a note to my aunt and you carry it back to her." The note read: "I'll come for supper to talk with you." He handed the note to the boy, who scampered off down the grass-covered earthen dike scurrying back to Rotterdam. Jon was a blond-haired, blue-eyed, strongly built young man. His muscles were firm from his work with his father at the stone quarry.

He carried no weapons, except his skinning knife in a sheath on the left side of his belt, but just his size and strength made him quite formidable. As the sun began setting in the west, over the English Channel, Jon began moving the herd of critters toward Rotterdam. After securing them in corrals for the night, he rode to his Aunt Julia's to see what she wanted. He knocked on the door and Aunt Julia opened the door saying, "Come in, Jon." John replied, "Aunt Julia, you sent for me?" "Yes, Jon, my three girls have been reading the Rotterdam Gazette and have corresponded to Mail-Order Bride Ads from America. They each have corresponded and replied to several men and I'm worried that they would go to America unsupervised." Julia continued, "All three girls have invitations and money to go to America from men in Santa Fe, New Mexico Territory. They have accepted money from one man each. That sounds like the Wild West to me, awfully wild. I wish you would accompany the girls and I would pay for your passage. Would you be willing to do this?" Her pleading eyes locked on him.

Jon replied, "I've been herding sheep and cattle for the community for a couple of years now and, while that's made me a fairly good horseman, I do get bored. So, yes, if I can be released by the city fathers and you'll pay my expenses, I'd be delighted for the adventure." Julia just beamed and she hollered, "Louise! Clara!

Rowena! You girls come down and see your cousin, Jon. Soon six feet were heard clamoring down the stairs from the upstairs bedrooms. In typical fashion of Dutch residences in town, the homes were very narrow, joined and stacked with two floors of bedrooms over the living area. Outside the home extended a beam to which a block and tackle could be attached to move furniture up to the appropriate floor, where it could be moved through an open window for placement in the room. This was necessary because the stairways are too narrow to move large furniture from floor to floor.

Years before, Aunt Julia had specifically requested Jon out of all his brothers to help her move in. This was due to his massive arms and shoulders and his extreme strength due to his work in the stone quarry. Julia previously asked Jon to install the furniture; his broad shoulders and narrow waist and hips resulted in his shoulders brushing each wall as he walked up the narrow staircase. As the girls alighted, Rowena squealed in terror as a rat ran across her toe. With exceptional hand and eye coordination, Jon flicked his skinning knife from his belt sheath with his right hand. An upside down flick of his wrist pinned the hapless rat to the shoe molding to the right of Rowena.

Julia said, "Sit down, girls. Jon, take a seat. Girls, Jon has agreed to accompany you to Santa Fe in

New Mexico Territory of the United States. I expect you to behave like ladies and listen to Jon's instructions, carrying them out without question. He will be there for your protection." Louise grimaced and said, "Mom! I'm a widow. I'm as old as Jon and certainly don't need protecting", she argued angrily. Rowena interrupted Louise, saying, "But, what about Clara and me? We are younger than you and Jon and have never been married. Our virtue certainly needs protection!" Clara joined in, "Yes, besides, I've read about the wild, wild west of the United States. Santa Fe is located west of the Mississippi River in the territory of New Mexico. There could be Mexican ruffians, Indian ruffians or other ruffians. Please do accompany us, Cousin Jon. Louise, did you see him kill that rat?" Jon replied, "I've never supervised anybody in my life. I have shot a fowling piece but never a pistol like they wear out west in America. I've never shot a rifle but I will try to learn and keep you safe. Sounds like a great adventure to me, if I don't have to argue with Louise over every issue or you other two over any order I may issue for your safety."

Louise ducked her head and peered through her eyelashes, "Well, maybe as a previously married woman, my virtue doesn't need protecting, but I do fear the Indians and the Mexicans so I would certainly listen to you, Jon, if you'd go with us," she cajoled. Julia clapped her hands together and exclaimed, "Well, it's all settled, then! I'll book passage for you on the "Night Wind" which sails on the morning tide."

Jon reflected on discovering how Louise had become pregnant out of wedlock back in Freesland, located in northern Holland.

Jon, while typically astride his horse, accidentally observed a man seducing Louise. Typical Dutch homes have lace curtains on the bottom half of the windows on the ground floor but Jon, astride his horse, could see above that curtain and observed what appeared to be Louise agreeably copulating with Sam on the sofa. Family rumors indicated that Sam Burt was the father of Louise's child. After three months, when Louise began to show as the baby grew within her, her mother to avoid the shame of unmarried motherhood hustled her off to Rotterdam. In the larger cities of Southern Holland, people were strangers even to their neighbors, who typically were Catholic or Muslim. From the family rumor mill, Louise claimed to be married to Sam Grabber and took the name Louise Grabber. Employing a Muslim lawyer in a back alley of Rotterdam, Louise arranged for her son, Lee, to be placed in a Catholic orphanage. She further arranged with this unethical lawyer to create a death certificate for her imaginary husband Sam Grabber.

Upon the birth of her son Lee, she immediately turned the child over to the Catholic orphanage when Lee was a week old. The nuns at the orphanage took Louise to Father James who informed her, "It will be necessary for you to supply funds for the care and feeding of the child annually, as you are not Catholic." Louise readily agreed. After a couple of months, when she regained her figure, she returned to Freesland. She and her sisters, who were not married, decided to respond to some ads in the Rotterdam Gazette, which Louise had brought back with her from Rotterdam. Louise was particularly taken with the ads from Santa Fe, so much so that she wrote to several men and accepted money from two of them so she would have a choice.

CHAPTER TWO

The next morning Jon met his aunt and her daughters at the gangplank to the Night Wind. The sky was just turning pink in the east as the ladies approached Jon, standing guard over their luggage. Julia was excited, hugging her daughters, weeping. She grabbed Jon's arm at the elbow and said, "Jon, I can hardly stand this. It scares me to think my daughters might marry someone in America and not come back to me." Jon replied, "Now, Aunt Julia, your daughters are going to marry and leave the nest someday. No sense weeping. I guess I'll go ahead and have the stevedores load this luggage on the ship." With his right arm, Jon waved to them to do so. Julia continued to weep, hugging each daughter in turn. Jon said, "All right girls, let's board." Jon turned and hugged his aunt good-bye. "So long, Aunt Julia. See you in a while." With a last gentle pat to Aunt Julia's shoulder, he turned on his heel. Upon reaching the main deck rail, he turned with the three girls to wave at their mother.

The ship captain, speaking loudly from the elevated quarterdeck, said, "Raise the main sail! Rudder to starboard." He walked the line fore and aft. The bow of the Night Wind swung into the main channel as the wind filled the canvas sail. Then the ship caught the gentle breeze and began accelerating toward the ocean. As the lock gates opened, the ship entered the English Channel. As the ship lurched gently into the channel, Louise, Rowena, Clara and Jon grabbed the ship's rail for support. Louise took an interest in the sailor handling the front mast. He was so handsome. The sea had become a little choppy with small white caps. Louise, with her left hand on the ship's rail, headed towards the handsome sailor, who was standing barefoot with legs spread for balance near the bow. Suddenly, the ship lurched down the trough of a wave, and recovered, causing the ship to pitch down and back up in a rhythm. Clara, Rowena and Jon all had to grab the handrail too. The first mate approached, under orders from the captain, to get those women to safety. The first mate addressed Jon, "Captain says the ladies should retire to their cabin until we are past the breakers," he said in a friendly manner. Jon responded, "Which cabin belongs to the ladies?" The mate replied, "Captain told me to place their luggage in the cabin across from his for their comfort and safety. On these small cutters, it is best to stay near the back as the short keel has them pitch and roll up front," and he pointed rearward to the quarterdeck. Jon replied, "Thanks" then said, "Louise, come back. Rowena and Clara, go to the cabin at the rear of the ship." "Dang it Jon, can't you see I'm talking to this handsome sailor?" Louise said. "Louise, I'm not going to argue with you. Get back in cabin number two for your own safety." Then the ship took a severe lurch and righted itself again and Louise lost her breakfast. With left hand on the rail and her right hand on the sailor's arm, she bent at the waist and vomited on the sailor's bare feet. The sailor jumped back with vomit dripping from his feet. So Louise had nothing to hold but the ship's rail. She quickly grabbed the rail with both hands. Jon went forward to grab Louise's arm and proceeded with her to the back of the ship. He helped her up the quarterdeck and to her cabin, maintaining his balance with widespread legs. Jon was glad he was wearing lace up boots to mid calf to strengthen his ankles. As he struggled for balance, one boot slipped on the wet deck. He nearly went to his right knee but caught his left hand on the frame of the cabin door and managed to stay upright. Louise had disappeared into the cabin, closing the door behind her. Across the gangway, the captain was standing barefoot at his cabin door. He indicated to Jon with a wave of his arm to join him in his cabin. Jon lurched over there and slipped and grabbed the doorframe to stay upright. The captain smiled and said, "You'd do better on the wet decks without those boots. The leather soles are slick when wet." Jon readily accepted the offered chair and proceeded to unlace and remove his wet boots. Thus, Jon became barefoot like the members of the crew. "Jon, I think your ladies would be safest if they dined with me. You all are invited to routinely dine in my quarters and avoid dining with my rough crew, as some of their language can be offensive. Besides, where they dine is one deck below this and it is darker, damper and more foul smelling." That's very kind of you, sir," Jon replied. "We will try to be on time for your mess call." The captain said as soon as the ladies had washed up, lunch would be served in his cabin. Surrounding the table were five other chairs besides the captain's. Jon noted that they were of heavy wooden construction, as was everything in the cabin. Jon also noticed a sextant on the sideboard under the porthole. The room was well lit with several portholes directly next to table and next to captain's berth. Jon took two strides across the aisle and called the girls to come eat. He then asked Louise if he could leave his boots in her cabin while they ate. He could see Louise with a clean but blue face. Louise said, "I don't think I can hold a thing down. Just let me lay here in this bed." "Very well." Jon responded. "Rowena and Clara, come."

As they crossed the gangway, the sailor who had been flirting with Louise approached her cabin. Jon held up his hand and walked between the sailor and Louise's cabin door and instructed the sailor to wait. "What seems to be the problem," the sailor replied.

"The ladies and I will be dining with the captain but sailors are not welcome to join us." Jon felt this guy was going to be trouble and he was right. The sailor produced a 44 Caliber Colt Peacemaker. Jon grabbed the man's wrist and shoved the hand skyward; with his other hand, Jon twisted the pistol from the sailor's hand. "Yow", the sailor howls, "that hurts". Hearing the scream, the captain's head poked out his cabin door. "What's going on here, Fred?" Jon interrupts. "I took the sailor's pistol away from him". Jon was so fast with eye hand coordination that he quickly disarmed the sailor without being harmed himself. As the captain stepped from his cabin, he was amazed to see the sailor holding his wrist and Jon holding the pistol by the barrel. He remarked, "I never saw one of my sailors disarmed by a passenger before. You must have an exceptional speed with your hands". The captain turned to the ladies and invited them in to be seated for lunch. When all of them were seated around the table, Jon, being a Mennonite, asked Captain Olmstead, "Would it be alright if I could ask the blessing before we eat?" "Yes, certainly," Olmstead responded.

"Lord, please bless this meal to the nourishment of our bodies and us to thy service. Keep us safe on this transatlantic voyage. Keep us safe in America. In Christ's name I Pray. Amen." As everyone was seated, the mess steward arrived and placed trays in front of each of the people seated at the captain's table. Cups of hot tea were placed before each of them. The captain faced Jon and said, "Look out this port hole next to the table. See that ship flying Jolly Roger black flag? That's the flag of a pirate ship. And see the white skull and cross bones on the black background. They no doubt intend to board us and rob us. Can you use a sword or a cutlass or even the revolver that you took from Fred?" "No, Sir, I am a member of the Mennonite church, and we do not believe in violence," Jon said. "Not even when you life is in danger or the women you are to protect? We will need all the hands on deck to protect against the pirates. Continue your meal, ladies, and Jon and I will go out on deck. I will try to teach him the element of self defense". The captain picked up the colt revolver and touched the cutlass at his waistband as he exited the door. Once upon deck, Olmstead placed the revolver in the sash behind his back. He then pulled the cutlass from the scabbard. He placed his left foot forward with his right knee bent and placed crossways behind him, sword elevated upward in his right hand. There upon he demonstrated a few defensive moves with the sword and handed the cutlass to Jon and said, "now you try it".

Jon being a natural athlete copied his moves precisely and adroitly. The captain smiled and told Jon that he had never seen a man with such a natural eye hand coordination and with a little practice, he could be an accomplished swordsman.

Next, the captain removed the colt peacemaker from his waistband. He turned and handed it to Jon and said, "Now, young man, let's see how you do with this pistol."

The Captain took Jon's hand in his and demonstrated how to cock the hammer. "Now squeeze the trigger, but do not jerk the trigger." Jon practiced shooting the pistol the rest of the day by shooting at garbage being thrown overboard by the cooks.

On the following day, Captain Olmstead addressed Jon at the supper table. "Young man, you may as well learn to shoot a rifle, too. As amazing as you are with a pistol already, the long gun is much better for shooting long distance. When you get out west of the Mississippi River, you won't find many grocery stores. You will need to be able to kill game to provide food for the table. Following our meal, I would like to show you how to use the 44 repeating Winchester that I have over there in my wardrobe."

"Yes, sir", Jon replied. "I'll be glad to learn to hunt. Any other advice that you may have on surviving in the wilderness will be appreciated."

After supper, they proceeded out on the quarterdeck with the 44 Winchester in hand. Captain Olmstead showed Jon how to load and lever a shell into the breach. He also showed him how to align his sights and reminded him, "Align the rear groove with the front sight. Hold your breath and gently squeeze, don't jerk the trigger." "CRASH!" The shot reverberated off the Captain's quarters and the can jerked where it floated in the ocean.

With all the firing, as Jon emptied the rifle's magazine in rapid fashion, the Pirates aboard the Pirate ship suddenly decided that would be an unhealthy ship to attack and turned back toward the English Coastline to find another ship to attack later.

This rifle and pistol firing practice was resumed after supper daily for three months.

By the time a second pirate ship appeared off the North American coastline, Jon was quite proficient with both weapons. Jon picked up the revolver as instructed and took a quick shot at the Jolly Roger flag on the rapidly approaching pirate ship, and at a distance of approximately

100 feet, a black round hole appeared in the center of the skull of the pirate's flag. The pirate ship continued rapidly closing in on the Cutter Night-Wind. The pirates were lined up next to the rail of the Night-Wind ready to board. Two held grappling hooks and tossed them over the rail of the Night-Wind, thereby snatching the two ships into a tight embrace. The lines were secured and the pirates jumped over the rail to the Night-Wind. Six cutlass-armed sailors as well as the Captain, the first mate and Jon, holding the Peacemaker, greeted them. With frantic swinging of cutlasses, most of the pirates were repelled immediately. But one slipped around to the left and charged at Jon. With only the Peacemaker for defense, Jon defended himself rapidly by fanning back the hammer with his left hand and triggering the revolver with his right index finger, and the Pirate was knocked flat on his back. Jon's quick response broke the attack of the pirates. The pirate Jon shot twitched once and died. His eyes sightlessly stared at the sky. The sailors from the Night-Wind continued to slash with their cutlasses as the pirates retreated to their ship.

The captain and the first mate jumped forward and chopped the lines connecting the grappling hooks with two swift chops, the two lines parted and approximately a foot separated the ships. The Captain rotated on his heel and pointed back at the helmsman and said, “Hard to Starboard”. The ships veered apart with the strong westerly wind. The Captain shouted, “Unfurl all the sails - main sail, top sail and foremast sail!” As the Night-Wind began gathering speed and soon out distanced the pirate ship, everyone relaxed. They were going toward the relatively safe area of Charleston Harbor. Jon offered the Peacemaker back to the Captain saying, “My goodness, I’m afraid I killed that pirate I shot.” “Lucky thing you did,” said the Captain. “It ended the attack by the pirates. We had already routed them with our cutlasses, but your blasting that pirate into hell took the fight out of them”.

CHAPTER THREE

Dawn was breaking in the east over the poop deck of the ship as they approached the Charleston Harbor. The rays of the morning sun sparkled brightly off of Fort Charleston Island. Olmstead skillfully guided the cutter in the main channel and began ordering for the sails to be lowered and stowed away. They glided effortlessly up to the Charleston docks and began departing the cutter. Jon descended the gangplank with a suitcase in each hand. He placed them on the dock and returned for the large brown traveling chest belonging to Louise. As he picked up the chest, his 44 Colt rubbed his ribs uncomfortably. Jon thought, "I wish I could find a smaller pistol that wouldn't take up so much room under my arm."

Jon and the sailors began carting the luggage down the gangplank to the dock. The ladies on the ship above were directing the sailors to handle the luggage with care as Jon stood below on the dock and carefully stacked the luggage for the brief carriage ride to the railway station. An open carriage stopped near Jon and the driver asked, "Do you need transportation to the railway, sir?" Jon replied, "That would be great." He began loading the luggage onto the backseat of the carriage as the three ladies exited the gangway. Jon spoke to them and said, "Let me go back and tell the Captain goodbye and thank him again. You ladies ride in the middle seat of the carriage. Your luggage is on the backseat. I'll ride on the front seat with the driver." Jon turned on his heel and re-entered the gangway and walked to the top where Captain Olmstead stood at the rail. Jon offered his hand and said, "Captain Olmstead, thank you for all the information on firearms and hunting and gathering nuts and berries. Maybe we will keep our bellies full now. Thanks, too, for the way that you avoided those pirates and kept us safe. That was mighty quick thinking to cut their grappling lines and get us safely here. I hope you have a safe return to Europe." Captain Olmstead responded, "Please keep this rifle and that Peacemaker revolver readily available. They are both 44 caliber weapons so one size cartridge will fit both. You will need the rifle to kill game and provide food west of the Mississippi River. The revolver will come in handy should you encounter ruffians. They then bid their farewells, and Jon joined his cousins at the carriage.

Jon sat next to the driver and said, "Let's go to the train station now." In just a few minutes, they were passing what seemed to be an old open-air market. Jon asked the driver why the platform was elevated. The driver explained that it was elevated because it was an old slave market and the slaves were auctioned off from the elevated platform so bidders in the crowd could better see them.

As they continued the carriage ride, Jon asked the driver, "Is there a gunsmith around here?" The driver pulled back on the reins and eased the carriage to a stop near the wooden sidewalk. He said, "Yes, sir, immediately to your right is one." Jon was shocked that guns were so plentiful in America and that gunsmiths were readily available. "Thanks," Jon said as he strolled across the sidewalk to the door of the gunsmith shop. Turning back to his cousins, he said, "Ladies, this 44 is heavy to tote and is rubbing my side raw. I will be right back."

Jon approached the counter to an older balding gray haired gentleman and asked, "Do you have anything smaller that I can carry," pulling the 44 from his shoulder holster and laying it on the counter. The old gray haired gentleman smiled, "Yes, sir, I have some of the late model Navy Colt 36 caliber. The Pony Express riders carried these, as they wanted a lighter weapon as they rode from Independence, Missouri to San Francisco, California. In fact, they couldn't stop to pour powder in the barrel and pack it down with a ramrod as they tried to escape attacking Indians or outlaws."

He continued, "Mr. Samuel Colt shaved the back off the cylinders and placed a metal strip in the back of the revolver to hold the copper jacketed cartridges of shells in place. However, he still only had five rounds in a cylinder, so the Pony Express riders often carried a couple of extra cylinders for quick reloading and change out. Now they had fifteen shots. I don't know if you realized that the Pony Express only lasted two or three years as Trans Continental Railroad quickly replaced them in 1859." The old balding gray haired gentleman smiled, admiring his own knowledge and cleverness.

Jon looked back at the man and appreciated the confusing information. This was all new to him. He then asked, "What has all this got to do with finding me a 36 caliber Colt Navy Pistol?" The old man replied, "Well, young man, as the Pony Express riders no longer carry the mail as the service ended eighteen years ago, I have a number of old Navy Colts available with spare cylinders. In fact, I have so many that I would trade you even for that 44 Colt here on the counter. I will also swap you the 44 caliber shoulder holster for a 36 Caliber shoulder rig with pockets for spare cylinders."

He continued, "Lastly, as your gun is new and mine are old, I will throw in a box of shells to be fair."

At the conclusion of their transaction, Jon started for the door and then turned back. He asked, "What do you have in the way of a light weight money belt?" The old man again smiled and reached below the counter producing a trim belt with three small pockets across the front and buckle to the side and cartridge loops in the back. It was tan in color and matched the coloration of the Colt Navy shoulder rig.

Now, sir, I have given you all I can give away in the trade so I will need a gold double eagle for the money belt."

Jon smiled and produced the twenty dollar gold piece from his right pants pocket.

"Fair enough. Is gold the only money acceptable in the United States or can you recommend a lighter weight currency?"

"Yes, sir, we have paper money called green backs," the old man smiled. "However, many people are leery of paper money since it devalued so greatly during the War of Yankee Aggression."

Jon thought, "These gentlemen from the confederate states are still fighting a war some 15 or 20 years later. It is almost like back in Freesland where many old-timers referred to Freesland being forced to join Holland back in 1400's."

Proud of all his transactions at the Gunsmith Shop, Jon rejoined his cousins on the carriage for the short remainder of their ride.

Soon they departed the carriage and began looking for the ticket office for the steam train to Chicago.

CHAPTER FOUR

As Jon approached the ticket counter, he deposited the baggage in the waiting area and told the ladies, "I'll be right back. You watch the luggage." Again, he approached the ticket counter and asked the clerk, "Is this the best route to Sante Fe, New Mexico, through Chicago?" The clerk responded, "Yes, sir. Most of our rail lines have been repaired since the Civil War some fifteen years ago. We did a lot of repairs on Sherman's bowties." Jon stared at the man and said, "What is a Sherman bowtie?" The Clerk responded, "When that Yankee General Sherman marched through Georgia from Atlanta to Savannah, he burned everything in sight and the rails would not burn. So, he bent the rails around trees to make them unusable. In the south, we refer to them as 'Sherman's bow ties'. You might see some of them off to the side the tracks overgrown with weeds where they still lie, but most of them were sent to Columbus, Georgia to the iron works for remelting and straightening. Then they were transported by ship down here to be reused.

The rail line is open all the way to Atlanta, even though Atlanta was burned about twenty-five years ago and is now mostly rebuilt. You should experience no trouble going through Atlanta, sir. From there, the tracks pass through Cleveland, Ohio, and have been repaired all the way through Chicago, Illinois.

Jon paid the fare for all four of them and the porter helped him load the luggage onto the luggage car. Louise, Rowena, and Clara all held out one small traveling case to carry onto the passenger car. Jon held their elbows as they climbed the stairs to the car while the porter was taking care of the luggage. Jon and Louise were facing backwards and Clara and Rowena were facing forwards as they took their seats. John lowered the small fold down table on the side wall to its support leg and said, "I hope they have some food on this train; I'm getting pretty hungry." Just then, the conductor walked down the aisle and asked for their tickets. After punching the tickets and returning them to Jon who was sitting on the aisle side, Jon asked, "Is there a dining car on this train?" The conductor responded, "No, sir. But we do have a store car two cars back where you can purchase fruits and vegetables and possibly some bread and cheese."

As the conductor moved on up the car, Jon said, "Louise, you and I, being the two oldest cousins, will go back and check on the food." They walked back to the store car and approached the counter to purchase some fruit, cheese and bread. There was no meat available. They returned to their car and shared their purchases with Clara and Rowena. Jon commented, I regret that we didn't stop at a restaurant before we got on the train, but I was anxious to get out of the big city."

With a slight lurch, the train began to leave the station. Each car went "Click, click, click, click" as the couplings pulled together. When the clicking reached their car, there was a lurch as the car began moving forward.

All four were exhausted from changing vehicles so often this day, so they dozed briefly until the conductor came down the aisle saying, "The Cleveland stop will be in one hour. There will be a half hour lay over where you will have an opportunity to dine in our railway cafe as we take on firewood and water for the steam engine." Jon was certainly glad that there was going to be a chance to eat something at the Cleveland train station. As the train slowed and stopped at the station, the four departed to the dining room, as did other passengers on the train. Jon and his cousins sat near the window so they could watch the train out of curiosity. He saw a horse-drawn wagon approach the tender car and observed several men moving pieces of tree limbs and wood sticks into the car. He noticed that all were cut to approximately two and a half feet in length, so that it would stack neatly on the tender. Meanwhile, other men were swinging a water trough from the water tank to the engine tank. A rope was pulled on the water tank and water came rushing down the chute into the engine's reserve tank. When this job was completed, the chute was swung out of the way and the horse-drawn cart was removed from the tender. As they were just finishing their meal of venison and grits, Louise asked, "What in the world are grits?" The waiter responded, "Mostly ground corn or hominy mixed with water." Louise said, "Not bad if we had some salt and pepper. Kind of bland right now." The conductor then shouted, "All Aboard! Five minutes to departure!" They began sliding out from their chairs and proceeding to the train where they re-entered their car. As Jon finished helping the ladies up the stairs, the conductor hollered, "Final call! All aboard that's going aboard to Chicago, Illinois." The conductor entered the platform on the back of the caboose, picked up the green lantern and waved it to the side where the engineer could see and yelled, "All aboard!" The engineer engaged the lever and the wheels began to turn as the train departed for Chicago, rapidly gaining speed. The fireman began transferring wood from the tender to the floor of the engine near the firebox. The fireman opened the door and threw three more logs on the fire. He closed the door of the firebox and the engineer pulled the rope hanging over his head, allowing the steam whistle to signal farewell to the city of Cleveland, Ohio.

The train hurled along at an amazing thirty miles per hour as they raced on toward Chicago. Clara said, "Cousin Jon, how fast were we going back there?" Overheard by the conductor, the conductor responded, "We reached a maximum of thirty-two miles an hour on that strait away back there." Clara gasped, "Do you think God wants us to travel that fast?" "This is nothing," the conductor said. "When you get west of the Mississippi River and you get on the high planes, some of those trains hit fifty miles an hour, if they don't hit a buffalo first. The front of the trains are equipped with cattle guards to shove buffalo or cattle out of the way should one get on the rail."

As the engine settled into a smooth thirty mile an hour trip across Ohio and Indiana, they were forced to stop three more times to replenish wood, water, and have three more meals. By this time, Louise was in a tizzy, her clothes were just black with smoke from the steam engine exhaust, where the smoke rose from the stack and blew back from the engine. Because of the heat, the windows were left partially opened on the car. The smoke came in the windows as it blew by, some of it landing on the passengers. Louise grimaced, "Now, look at what a mess we're in. Will we have a chance to clean up before we meet the men who have sent for us?" Jon reassured all three of the ladies, "When we get to Independence, you should get a chance to wash up some. But I would wait for a bath until after we get off the train to Sante Fe, because the conductor explained to me that there is not much wood west of the Missouri River in the area known as the Great Plains. We will be running on coal, which the conductor told is a lot dirtier burning than wood and will mess up your clothes and face. We will all look black when we get to Sante Fe. We will check into a hotel and get a bath before we meet your men."

Jon proved to be right. Upon leaving Independence, where the coal and water was replenished, a dirty foursome enjoyed a good meal of luscious, delicious, huge beefsteaks. As they departed for Topeka, a herd of buffalo was on the tracks near the town of Atchison, Kansas. The train was forced to stop as the critters ambled across the track in their own good time. When the last of the buffalo herd left the rails, the engineer pulled the whistle cord and engaged the drive wheel lever. They proceeded on to Atchison in a cloud of black smoke.

Jon took his seat on the velveteen cushions of the passenger coach. He and Clara sat facing Rowena and Louise. Directly across the aisle, also facing Jon was a beautiful olive skinned part Seminole maiden named Sonia. Every time Sonia glanced at Jon, he was glancing admiringly at her. A bit disconcerted, Sonia tugged at her skirt to make sure her knees were covered down to her ankles. She noticed Jon staring at her ankles. Jon was thinking, "My, those are beautiful slim ankles. I wonder what the rest of the leg looks like." Sonia tugged her dress down just a little farther and tucked her feet under the hem of her skirt. She blushed and looked quickly out the window to her right. In doing so, her eyes darted over the face of a stranger facing her across the seat. This bearded gentleman mistook her glance for admiration and quickly changed seats and sat next to her. He placed his arm around the back of her shoulder. He said, "Hey, darlin'. You sure are a pretty Indian princess." He hugged her shoulder. Sonia was alarmed and glanced at Jon, her eyes pleading for help. Jon, who had been watching this exchange, said sharply, "Hey, mister, don't be pawing that lady!" The man returned Jon's angry glance with a hate stare of his own and rebutted, "What business is it of yours? Mind your own business if you know what's good for you."

Sonia's eyes continued to plead for help from Jon, thus encouraging Jon to reach across the aisle. Placing his hand on the seat facing Sonia, he moved into the aisle, standing to his full six-foot height and two hundred pound frame. The 36 Navy Colt was still in his shoulder rig beneath his jacket. When the gentleman jumped up to return his angry stance, he accidentally knocked Sonia in the jaw. She grimaced and leaned away from him towards the window, covering the growing red bruise on her chin with her left hand. This really upset Jon. "I might cut this man, or possibly shoot him," Jon thought. But, being a good Mennonite, he decided to limit his violence. He wouldn't let the woman be abused, so he pulled the Navy Colt from his shoulder rig and struck the man against the side of his head and brought him down to his knees. When the man landed on his knees, he grabbed for support and once again, his hands fell in Sonia's lap. Since he inappropriately touched Sonia on the thigh, Jon was further angered. With his pistol in his right hand, he struck at the stranger again with a quick short jab with his left hand. It connected with the man in his jaw and he dropped to the floor, out cold. As Jon replaced his gun into his holster, Sonia was overcome with relief. She jumped up and impulsively hugged Jon across the chest. "Oh, thank you for stopping that foul smelling man from bothering me," she said. Jon was pleased by the softness of her breasts against his chest and her pleasant smell. He was uncertain what to do, though pleased with her attention. Being a total stranger to him, he took her by the hands and gently led her to his seat beside his cousins and said, "Glad to have helped you, ma'am. Why don't you sit over here with my cousins while I drag this man to the end of the car." Jon grabbed the back of the man's collar and dragged him to the back of the car, throwing him down without gentleness. Then, he went back and sat in the seat that had previously been occupied by Sonia. Sonia continued to look admiringly and appreciatively at Jon, which made him nervous. To avoid her beautiful hazel eyes, he stared out the window to his right. This first encounter would prove to be prophetic, as they would continue to see much of each other on their way to Sante Fe. In fact, romance would blossom as they admired each other.

CHAPTER FIVE

Changing trains in Chicago, Clara, Louise, Rowena and Jon entered their next train, going through St. Louis to Topeka, Kansas. They were in the passenger car just ahead of the dining car. The four again, sat facing each other. Jon was seated next to Clara. After the train picked up speed, the conductor came down the aisle saying, "The dining car will be serving lunch for the next hour." Jon addressed his cousins, "Are you as hungry as I am? Let's go to lunch first. We can see the Illinois countryside from the windows."

As the train went 'clickety, clickety, clack' from the train wheels hitting the tracks, the four walked to the car behind them. They crossed the platform from the passenger car to the dining car. Jon held the dining car door open with his left hand, while extending his right arm to his cousins, so they could make their way across the metal plate between the two cars. They sat in the first booth to the left and were approached by a waiter. The waiter took their orders and returned to the galley end of the car. Before placing their order, he stopped at the table of a beautiful blonde who was sitting alone. She glanced repeatedly at the good-looking Jon and then said to the waiter, "I hate to eat alone. Could I move down and join those five at the other end of the car?"

The waiter saw that there were plenty of other tables that she could move to, so he knew Jon was the attraction. He smiled and said to her, "If you wish to join the good looking gentleman in that booth, may I place your order at the same time? Tell me your name and I'll ask the gentleman if you may join him." "My name is Sharon Sonbourn of Richmond, Virginia," she answered him in her southern drawl. The waiter placed the order with the cook and returned to the other end of the car where he addressed Jon, "Sir, that attractive blonde-headed lady seems to have taken a shine to you. Her name is Sharon Sonbourn of the Virginia Sonbourns, she informed me. She does not like dining alone and would like to join you. What do you think?"

Jon didn't have a chance to respond before Louise jumped in with, "There are already five of us at this table. I don't know where she would sit. Louise had anger in her voice. Jon waved his hand dismissively and responded, "If that table across the aisle is not taken, I'll move over there and dine with her." Louise glared at Jon and said, "Don't be paying for her meal with our money."

Jon responded, "Louise, I brought some money that your mother provided, but I also brought my last two weeks pay with me, so hush."

He proceeded across the aisle and sat at the table by himself. The waiter went to Sharon's table and said, "Ma'am, the gentleman would be glad to have you sit at his table. Sharon smiled at him with her perfect white teeth. With a glimmer in her blue eyes, she said politely, "Thank you, sir. That was so kind of you. Please bring my meal to his table." She then proceeded down the aisle to join Jon, while Sonia glared at this new development. After joining him, they carried on a pleasant conversation while waiting on the delivery of their meal. Across the aisle, Louise glared with anger because she did not get her way. For punishment for his independent decision, she gave Jon the silent treatment for the rest of the day.

When Sharon's grits and eggs and Jon's eggs and bacon arrived, they continued to smile at one another as she very daintily placed the food in her mouth. Jon was impressed with her table manners. Before eating, Jon had prayed silently over his meal. She noticed that his hands were folded on the table and his eyes were closed. Sharon asked, "Were you praying?" "Yes, I was giving thanks to the Lord," Jon responded. This impressed Sharon, whose five brothers simply would have wolfed down their food, while not stopping to thank the Lord for his bounty. Jon said, "I'm a Mennonite, although a bit of a back slider. I've had several violent encounters in our trip from Holland. We are supposed to be non-violent, but I have been charged with the care of my three cousins. I have found it necessary to come to their defense several times." Sharon was interested; you could see it in her eyes. "Won't you tell me about that, sir? What did you say your name was?" "Jon is my name," he responded. "And the waiter said your name is Sharon, is that right?" "Sharon Sonbourn of the Virginia Sonbourns. My grandfather had a large plantation before the Civil War, some twenty years ago, but that estate was fairly ravaged during the war. My father found it necessary to become a soldier in the hated Union Army. The Carpetbaggers were charging such high taxes that we could not keep up the estate, with the slaves being freed. We had to pay for help and taxes. He joined the union army to support his family." As they talked, Sharon was quite impressed with Jon and rubbed the calf of his leg with her foot, flirting with him under the table. This did not please Sonia at all. Louise also noticed Sharon rubbing Jon's leg with her foot under the table and thought it was a good way to get a man's attention, so she tucked it away in the back of her mind for future use. Meanwhile, Jon was aroused by her attention and blushed red. He was thinking un-Mennonite-like thoughts, so he twisted his body to put his legs out into the aisle and away from her foot. Jon continued his blushing, but Sharon demurely looked down into her coffee cup, ignoring Jon's discomfort, like her planned event was an accident. The waiter approached the table, nearly stumbling over Jon's feet, so Jon put them back under the table. The waiter asked, "How did you want this, one bill or two?" Jon responded, "One, sir." Sharon said in a coquettish southern drawl, "On, no. I'll pay my own. That wouldn't be fair inviting myself over to be your guest and then have you pay for my meal." Jon said, "Think nothing of it. It was a pleasure sharing your company." The waiter took the money from Jon, thus settling the argument. Sharon placed her hand over Jon's thanking him, "That was so sweet. " She thought to herself, "My, he is one handsome blonde headed giant." And then aloud she said, "You said you were from Holland? They certainly grow men big there and you sure do look strong," she flattered. Jon blushed again and responded, "I'm from Freesland, the northern part of Holland, and generally the men are over six feet tall. We are typically blonde and blue eyed, but I am by no means a giant among men from Freesland." Sharon's coquettish gleam in her eye matched her brilliant white smile and cooed, "Well, I would feel safe being protected by you, that's for sure. Your cousins are certainly lucky." She patted Jon's hand again affectionately. Jon felt the heat rise into his face again and knew he was blushing. To change the subject, he asked, "Did you say you are going all the way to Sante Fe as we are?" Sharon smiled and responded, "Yes." Jon then invited her to be part of his protection detail adding, "You can join us as we leave the train to find the hotel. I certainly would not mind protecting you and making sure you get there safely." Sharon gave him another squeeze of his hand and said, "You are sooooooooo sweeeeeeeeet!" She then exited the car to return to the passenger coach.

Sonia saw her competition leave and proceeded to join Jon across the aisle asking, "May I sit here as the other table is quite crowded?" Louise observed this and thought "another forward woman." Jon stood and greeted Sonia, offering her a seat with the gesture of his arm. "Yes, please join me, Sonia," he said. Sonia was pleased at his gallantry that he stood for a lady and she took the seat that he offered. As the beautiful landscape flashed by in the window, the sun reflected off the green trees and flashed glowingly against her olive complexion. Jon was suddenly in love again. Jon said, "Sonia - that is your name, is it not? Did you tell me that you were going to Sante Fe, as we are?" Sonia smiled, showing her pearly whites and answered, "If I can remember that you are Jon, you should be able to remember that I am Sonia. I saw that woman leaving your table. Were you too smitten with her to remember my name? Yes, I am going to Sante Fe to visit my uncle."

Jon thought, "How do you choose between so many beautiful women in America, plus the beautiful maidens back in Holland. What's a guy to do," he worried.

Later, as Jon departed for the train to Independence, Missouri, he found that he had not three, but five women - his three cousins and then the two that he had met on the train. As the west was so shy of women that they had to run ads in Holland newspapers for mail order brides, Jon with his collection of five women drew quite a lot of attention. "Must surely be a Mormon," one man thought. Another man approached him as he walked down the platform with five women trailing behind him and said angrily, "You damn Mormon. Five wives? No wonder the rest of us have to send out for them through the mail!" The man swung from the hip with his right hand from the waist and aimed for Jon's jaw. Jon was already alert due to the man's belligerent scowl, so he easily dodged the blow. The man was thrown off balance and fell at his feet. He could have easily kicked the man who fell on his face, but his religious teaching taught against that. Instead, he stopped, stooped down and picked up the gentleman's hat and offered him a hand up, giving him his hat. He responded, "I'm no

Mormon, sir. I am a Mennonite. Three are my cousins and two are my new friends. Please stand aside and let us pass." John nudged him aside with his elbow and moved past. His five-woman entourage followed him until they reached the open-air café. Jon asked the ladies if they would like to stop and sit under the awning and enjoy some cool lemonade. They all thought that was an excellent idea and seated themselves at a round table. Sharon maneuvered to get a seat next to Jon and Sonia took the one at his other side. Louise glowered and said, "Do you two ladies think Jon is a mail-order husband or something?" This she said with spiteful arrogance. The naturally quiet Sonia, in the tradition of her Indian fore bearers, retained a stoic, non-committal silent demeanor. Her emotions were unreadable to Louise, who just saw a blank expression. However, Sharon responded in her drawl, "I didn't mail-order Jon, but I'd be glad to send him a letter. He would be quite a catch." Sonia kept her own counsel, but thought the same way.

As darkness began to descend on the car, the conductor came through lighting oil lamps at both ends of each car. After he left the car, Jon noticed that one of the oil lamps was smoking severely. In fact, the globe was entirely black, emitting very little light.

Jon then got up and turned the wick down in the oil, extinguishing the flame. He touched the globe to remove it and found it to be very hot to the touch, nearly burning his fingers. He reached in his back pants pocket and produced a neckerchief folded neatly in a square. This he used to grasp the top of the globe pulling it from its wire retainer. Lifting the globe carefully over Sonia's head, he handed it across the aisle to Sharon asking, "Would you mind wiping out the globe with my neckerchief so we can get some light from it." As Jon returned to the wick, he pulled his skinning knife out from his belt, raising the wick from the oil and trimmed the ragged top edge off with his knife. Behind him, Sharon said, "I'll do my best, but I have never had to clean one. Our servants always handled this messy work back in Virginia." Sonia, sitting next to her, said, "Give it to me. I'll clean it up for you. I'm not afraid of a little work." She thought, " Jon won't be very impressed with prissy Miss Sharon. A man in the western frontier needs a woman to work beside him, not one who expects her work to be done by servants."

She was right. Jon was not impressed with the prissiness of the Virginia aristocratic lady. As Sonia handed the globe back to Jon, she purposely rested her hand on his a little longer than necessary. Jon felt the warmth of her hand on his and noticed what an excellent job she did cleaning the interior of the lamp's globe and told her so as he replaced it in its retainer.

Just then, the conductor returned from the back of the train. As he approached, Jon said, "Would you mind relighting this lamp for us? It was smoking and I trimmed the wick and Sonia cleaned the globe." The conductor replied, "Yes" and proceeded to light it immediately and left the car through the front sliding door and the lamp glowed beautifully.

As dawn broke, the train was approaching Cairo, Illinois. Jon suggested they get off the train to stretch their legs and have a cup of coffee as the fireman was scheduled to replenish coal and water.

Jon and his entourage returned to their awaiting train car and Jon helped each lady by holding her elbow as they ascended the steps to the car. Both Sonia and Sharon greeted Jon's courtesy with a flirtatious grin.

CHAPTER SIX

Reverend Alex Johnson boarded the train in Cairo, Illinois, headed for a scheduled camp meeting at Independence, Missouri as a Circuit Riding Preacher. He had put his swayback nag in the horse car and was toting his saddle and saddlebags containing his Bible and prepared text. He dropped them on the floor at the end of the dining car and was seated at a table near Jon and the ladies.

Once seated, an active eight year old girl named Camden, trailed by her grandmother Patsy Jones, who had previously attended his camp meeting at the Ohio River Crossing. Camden, came up behind the preacher and asked in an excited voice, "Reverend Johnson, what if someone stole your saddle, would you forgive them and just turn the other cheek?" Her grandmother, correcting her said, "Don't be interrupting Reverend Johnson's meal, Camden." Smiling at Camden, he said, "Oh, that's all right, I eat way too much anyway. In fact, my horse is getting swayback from me riding him over all of Missouri and Illinois," he joked.

Camden continued, "Well, Preacher Man, I remember at the camp meeting when you told us that Jesus said we should turn the other cheek and to forgive our enemies.

Does that mean I have to forgive those Indians who killed my parents?" Preacher Alex explained, "Camden, you told me that your grandmother now takes care of you since you lost your mother and father. She will be there for you now. I know you miss your parents, but to spend all your time hating will burn you up inside. It will hurt you more than it will hurt the Indians. I think that was what Jesus was telling us. Hate is a wasted effort. Love is far more important and your grandmother will now provide that love for you," the Preacher concluded.

As Reverend Alex turned back to the table, Louise asked, "Reverend, I couldn't help but overhear you talking to the little girl. Could I speak with you privately, please?" as she pointed to the other end of the dining car. Reverend Johnson nodded 'yes' and proceeded to another table followed by Louise.

In a whisper, Louise said, "Reverend Alex, I am worried about my soul. You see, I was pregnant out of wedlock back in Holland. The father of my young son

Lee is a Catholic priest who lied to me about marrying me. Now Lee is in a Catholic orphanage in Amsterdam. Because I am not Catholic, I am required to pay an annual stipend to the orphanage for his care. I have come to America to find a rich rancher husband to help me pay that amount. Is this a sin?"

"First of all," Reverend Alex said, "the Old Testament is filled with stories about children born out of wedlock, even about prostitution. So I know God forgives if you ask him to." He continues, "If you intend for this rancher to help you with expenses for a child not his, you must be honest up front and not lie to him." Satisfied, Louise smiled and returned to the other end of the dining car to join the others.

Jon said, "Wait a minute, please Reverend. I have a question for you, too." And Jon proceeded to the private end of the dining car to confer with Reverend Johnson.

Upon being seated across the dining table from the Reverend, Jon stated, "I am a Mennonite – not a Methodist; but I would appreciate your opinion on my recent actions. You see, I am a member of a non-violent religious sect. However, since I left Holland, it has been one violent encounter after another. Crossing the Atlantic, I killed a pirate with a bullet from my revolver and I fought a sailor with my fists to keep him away from Louise. My Aunt Julia has asked me to escort her daughters to Santa Fe, New Mexico and to assure their safety. This has proven to be a challenge to my religious beliefs. What advice can you give to me?" Reverend Johnson responded, "You come from a civilized nation back in Europe. Unfortunately, the open sea is a lawless area as are the western territories of the United States that you are now entering. It is one thing to be non violent when we have police or military protection. As you have been assigned the responsibility for the safety of your cousins, you may have to put on a new hat as their protector. Jesus did teach non- violence; yet, the Bible is filled with stories of violence where men must defend their way of life for their beliefs. From this point in your journey westward, each man is a law unto himself. There will be no one to protect you or your cousins except your own self-defense. My advice, therefore, is to turn the other cheek when you can so as not to provoke others. To get these ladies safely to Santa Fe, I am afraid you will continue to be required to use violence when necessary. I believe God will understand your love for your cousins."

With this response, the train began lurching to a stop at Independence Station.

Reverend Alex Johnson stated in his deep bass voice, "I will be holding a camp meeting tonight on the eastern side of the Missouri River where the railroad tracks cross the river. You will see the bond fire. You all come. Everyone is welcome." Then he turned to Camden and her grandmother and asked, "Can either of you sing?" Both women grinned broadly and Mrs. Jones said, "We both sing in the choir in our church back home. Why, can we help you?" "Yes" he said. "I would like for Camden to sing 'The Old Rugged Cross' at the conclusion of my sermon as the hymn of invitation, and Mrs. Jones, would you open with 'Amazing Grace'?" She responded with a chuckle, "Well, yes, I'll be glad to sing, but you know with no music, AMAZING could have ten syllables."

Jon said, "Having previously missed your Ohio River Crossing meeting, we would like to attend this one. I'll help you set up your campfire if you wish, Reverend."

"Yes, please," answered Reverend Alex. And the two men proceeded downhill to the Missouri River's edge just right of the trestle. Some local men had been expecting the Circuit Riding Preacher with anticipation and already had a stack of firewood prepared for his use. They also had used a cross cut saw to cut large pieces of tree trunk to make seats for the ladies, most of whom would be wearing dresses.

When Jon and Alex arrived at the prepared campfire site, building a campfire was no longer necessary. All they needed was to set the pile of wood ablaze at dusk. Yet, Preacher Johnson made some last minute adjustments in the tree stump seating prepared for the ladies. Jon helped him.

As the citizens of Independence began drifting down the hill, Jon's entourage joined the local people in the camp meeting. Reverend Johnson welcomed all the visitors and invited all the ladies to be seated and then said in his loud bass voice, "Lord, we pray your presence be with us at this camp meeting tonight as we come to praise your name. AMEN."

"We have a very special guest tonight. Mrs. Jones, will you come forward and lead us in *'Amazing Grace*?" As this beautiful hymn was being sung, the presence of the Lord was felt among the crowd as she began to sing.

AMAZING GRACE

[1]*Amazing Grace, how sweet the sound,*
That saved a wretch like me.
I once was lost but now am found.
Was blind but now I see.

Twas grace that taught my heart to fear,
And grace my fears relieved;

1 "Amazing Grace", Copied from United Methodist Hymnal

How precious did that grace appear
The hour I first believed.

The Lord has promised good to me,
His word my hope secures;
He will my shield and portion be
As long as life endures.

When we've been there ten thousand years
Bright shining as the sun.
We've no less days to sing God's Grace
Than when we first begun.

As the service continued, Reverend Johnson, knowing that less than half the men could read, asked Jon to read the *Apostles Creed*, as he recalled having seen Jon reading his Bible earlier.

Jon graciously obliged and began to read:

[2]*I believe in God, the Father Almighty,*
Maker of Heaven and Earth.
And in Jesus Christ, His only Son, our Lord;
Who was conceived by the Holy Spirit,
Born of the Virgin Mary,
Suffered under Pontius Pilate,

---

2 "The Apostle's Creed, Copied from United Methodist Hymnal

Was crucified, dead and buried.
The third day he rose from the dead;
He ascended into Heaven,
And sitteth at the right hand.
Of God the Father Almighty
From thence he shall come
To judge the quick and the dead.
I believe in the Holy Spirit,
The holy catholic church,
The communion of saints,
The forgiveness of sins,
The resurrection of the body,
And the life everlasting. AMEN

Reverend Johnson then began his sermon. "My sermon tonight is *It's Easy to Become a Christian, but Harder to Live as a Christian*."

[3] *The mark of a great leader is the demands he makes upon his followers. Jesus spoke of the necessity of total commitment – even to the point of death. He conveyed this in no uncertain terms when he said to his disciples, "You must take up you cross and follow*

3 Excerpts with permission from sermon of Reverend John Alexander, Pastor of Trinity On The Hill United Methodist Church, LaGrange, Georgia, 2010

me." Why was Jesus so harsh? He knew what lay ahead:

- *Andrew died on a cross*
- *Bartholomew was flayed alive*
- *James (son of Zebedee) was beheaded*
- *The other James (son of Alphaeus) was beaten to death*
- *Matthew was slain by the sword*
- *Peter was crucified upside down*
- *Phillip was hanged*
- *Simon was crucified*
- *Thaddeus was shot to death with arrows*

Only John made it through alive but he was exiled to a small island in the middle of the Mediterranean Sea.

The demands that Jesus makes upon those who would follow him are extreme. Christianity is not a Sunday morning religion. It is a hungering after God to the point of death if need be. It shakes our foundations, topples our priorities, pits us against friend and family, and makes us strangers in this world. We sing, "What a Friend We Have in Jesus." But, we must understand that on many occasions, Jesus is not our friend but our adversary. We learn in this text that a large crowd was traveling with Jesus. Now, in large crowds, you will find many motives. Some in this crowd are following because they have seen Jesus feed a multitude of people and they are waiting to be fed. Some are following because they have heard of Jesus' ability to heal and they are waiting for an opportunity to approach him and be healed. Still others are following for the excitement. It is safe to say that only a few are truly committed to this itinerant preachers teaching. Aware of their multiplicity of motives, Jesus turns to the crowd and tells them what is involved in a true commitment. At this moment the crowd learns, and we do also, what it takes to follow Jesus.

I. We must establish our priorities. Too often we allow things to stand in the way of that which we consider important. Jesus said, "If any man would come after me, let him deny himself and take up his cross and follow me." He comes to us as one to be obeyed.

II. Secondly, we must count the cost. "Suppose", Jesus said, "one of you wants to build a tower over your vineyard so you can keep a lookout for thieves who might want to steal your harvest. Before you build, what is the first thing you will do? Will you not, Jesus said, first sit down and estimate how much it will cost you to build the tower? Don't let it be said of you, dear friends: He began to build but was not able to finish. She followed the teacher but did not learn the lesson. He followed the Lord but did not carry his cross. Yes, count the cost.

III. <u>We must be willing to pay the price</u>. Jesus told the crowd, "Any of you who are not willing to give up everything cannot be my disciple." Let me ask you, could it be any clearer than that? Jesus spells out the extremely high cost of discipleship. It will cost all that you have.

Abraham gave up his Son.
Moses gave up Pharaoh's court.
Peter gave up his family and their fishing business.
Matthew gave up the profession of a tax collector.
Paul gave up his prestigious position as a Pharisee.

Now unless you are called into full time Christian ministry, you will not be asked to do as these men have done. But none of us can escape the need to establish our priorities, count the cost, and pay the price.

In closing, I have often wondered what would have become of the church at large if Jesus' disciples had not made those ultimate sacrifices and put down their crosses.

Next, Preacher Alex turned to eight year old Camden. "We have some special music by Camden Jones at this time." Camden came forward, and in her angelic voice sang 'The Old Rugged Cross'.

[4]*On a hill far away, stood an old rugged cross,*
The emblem of suffering and shame.
And I love that old cross where the dearest and best
For a world of lost sinners was slain.

Oh that old rugged cross, so despised by the world
Has a wondrous attraction for me;
For the dear Lamb of God left his glory above
To bear it to dark Calvary.

To the old rugged cross I will ever be true,
Its shame and reproach gladly bear;
Then He'll call me someday to my home far away,
Where His glory forever I'll share.

Chorus: So I'll cherish the old rugged cross,
Till my trophies at last I lay down;
I will cling to the old rugged cross,
And exchange it some day for a crown.

4 "The Old Rugged Cross" Copied from United Methodist Hymnal

The rough men on the riverside whooped, hollered, cheered and stomped exuberantly for Camden. She was the hit of the evening.

Finally, Reverend Johnson stated, "I have a canteen of water here on this log. If any one of you feels the desire to commit to Christ tonight, I will be happy to baptize you at your request. Don't worry about running out of water," he chuckled as he pointed back to the river behind him. "We Methodist will baptize by sprinkling, pouring or immersing, as you desire.

"Let us end our camp meeting tonight with the Lord's Prayer." Knowing most could not read, he read from Matthew 6:10-14. Everyone feeling revived and renewed from hearing the word listened intently with heads bowed as he read.

5 *The Lord's Prayer*

Our Father, who art in Heaven,
Hallowed be Thy name.
Thy kingdom come, Thy will be done
On earth as it is in Heaven.
Give us this day our daily bread;
And forgive us our trespasses as we forgive those

5 "The Lord's Prayer", Copied from The King James Version of the Holy Bible
Matthew 6:10-14

Who trespass against us.
And lead us not into temptation,
But deliver us from evil
For thine is the kingdom, and the power
And the glory forever. AMEN

At the conclusion of the Lord's Prayer, the crowd started dispersing back to Independence. Jon was leading his entourage back up the hill to the train station when four men confronted him. The leader of the group said, "You dang Mormon, you don't deserve five wives. Come on boys, let's get us a woman each."

As the four men aggressively approached Jon, Reverend Alex observed the looming confrontation. Jon knew he could handle two or three, but four was a bit much; so he was delighted when Reverend Alex sided him. Reverend Alex was a bear of a man and, as a man of the cloth, Jon was surprised when he knocked two men to the ground quickly with a right and a left. Jon brandished his Navy Colt from beneath his jacket and discouraged the final two. The fight was over just about before it started. Jon holstered his pistol and reached his right hand out to shake hands with Reverend Alex and said, "Thanks for your non-violent intervention, preacher!"

CHAPTER SEVEN

Jon and his five women entourage boarded the third passenger car of the train named "The City of Sante Fe". Jon seated the ladies. Louise and Clara sat in the first seat to the left of the front sliding door to the carriage. Sharon and Sonia sat behind them in the second seat to the left on the maroon velvety cushion. Behind them was Jon on the aisle and on the window side was Rowena. The conductor came down the aisle collecting tickets. He was dressed in a black broadcloth suit with his nametag firmly attached to his right pocket. It said 'Red'. As he approached, Jon held up all six tickets. The conductor punched all six and handed them back to Jon.

Jon said, "How fast will we be traveling on this leg of our trip?" Red replied, "I expect we will hit as fast as 50 miles an hour on the straight away." Up ahead, Louise overheard them and shouted, "Fifty miles an hour! Do you think God wants us to go that fast?" Conductor Red answered, "Well, I'm not sure about God, but my biggest concern is those buffalo wandering across the track up ahead." He then pulled the emergency cord and immediately notified Engineer Dave that there was an imminent problem. Luckily, the engineer was awake and had seen the buffalo at the same time and had begun slowing the train.

The Engineer Dave remarked to the Fireman Bill, "This is a small herd and should be out of the way soon. I remember back before the hide hunters killed off all the buffalo they were in the millions; now the herds are only in the hundreds. So I guess we won't be running that late getting to the [6]Harvey House Restaurant at the next stop."

Engineer Dave continued talking to Fireman Bill, "You couldn't get a decent meal on this railroad until Fred Harvey open his restaurant. He cleaned up the food establishments along the Atchison Topeka Sante Fe Railroad. The food was slop but now it is excellent. Mr. Harvey hires only pretty girls with the best reputations to serve the food."

"In fact," he said, "these girls have to live in his dormitories and wear his uniform which is a black dress down to no more than one inch above the floor. I understand, too, that the dress must be covered with a white apron to no more than four inches above the floor.

---

6 Fred Harvey of England established the Harvey House Restaurant with his "Harvey Girls" in 1875 through the 1890's.

I have been told that if they get even a drop of gravy on that apron, they must change it immediately!" He continues, "Furthermore, all the girls must be single and not in a romantic relationship and must not court the customers or the train employees. Now I think that last rule was a big mistake," he grimaced.

CHAPTER EIGHT

As the steam engine approached Sante Fe, the engineer shrilled his whistle in a greeting of, "Hello, the train is coming in!"

There was quite a crowd of cattlemen and cowboys and other Sante Fe citizens on the train platform, smiling and waving as the train approached. There were a number of Mexican/Spanish people waiting along with the Anglos. Jon looked out at the smiling faces and smiled and waved back. When the passenger car stopped near the center of the train platform, Jon said, "Let me step off first and settle our luggage. Then, you ladies come down."

Once he had the luggage on the platform, he signaled with a wave of his arm to come on down the steps and all three of his cousins joined him. However, his two new friends, Sonia and Sharon, stood to the side slightly apart near their own luggage. Jon eyed all the men approaching and briefly touched his Navy Colt in his shoulder holster under his jacket to reassure himself that it was still there just in case he needed it to defend his cousins. Four men approached instead of three. The first tipped his hat and approached Clara and in a courtly bow, he said, "Miss Clara, my name is Steve. With that blond hair, I assume you are Clara Roosma. We have been corresponding for some time. Will you join me for lunch here at the Harvey House Restaurant?" She grasped his big hard working hand in both of her delicate ones and responded, "Steve, I'm delighted to meet you at last. I would be happy to have a meal with you."

The second gentleman approached the brunette Rowena and doffed his hat. Then he asked, "Miss Rowena, I presume?" Rowena responded, "Samuel?"

"Yes, Rowena, I am Samuel." Flashing her eyes, Rowena said, "You are much taller than I imagined and certainly more handsome than I expected."

The final two gentlemen approached Louise, jostling one another with their elbows. The shorter of the two said, "Miss Louise?"

The taller gentleman, Claude Steeler, shoved the other gentleman aside with his elbow and said, "Now wait just a minute, sir. I sent money to Louise for her trip to America to meet me. And as this is the last lady of the three, it must be Louise."

The smaller one, Christopher Rodriquez said, "Now you wait just a minute, Claude. I sent money, too. Louise must be waiting for me," as he shoved him back.

Louise responded, "Now gentlemen, you didn't expect me to come all the way across the Atlantic without some choice of escort, did you?" She smiled with evil in her eyes.

Jon stepped forward and placed himself between the two men and one hand on each man's chest. His left hand rested on Christopher's chest and his right on Claude's chest as he said, "Gentlemen, I am sure that we can work this out without resorting to violence." Then Jon turned his back on them and faced Louise. He asked, "Louise, did you accept Night Wind passage from both men?"

Louise responded, "Jon, I'm sure that my mother Julia gave you enough money to pay one of these gentlemen back once I have made my selection." Then Louise turned to face the two men and addressed them with, "Well, Claude. You are certainly the larger of the two, but Christopher, you are one handsome man." She buttered up both men, and then she said, "Which one of you can better keep me in the style to which I would like to become accustomed? Chris, how large is your ranch? How many cattle do you own?" Then turning to face Claude, she asked the same questions of him.

Chris responded, "Out here, its control of the water rights that is important. Most of the land is owned by the federal government and considered open-graze land. Therefore, I can't really say how many acres I own. I have filed on a homestead of 160 acres covering two artesian well sites. I can't say how much free-graze is available, but literally thousands of acres. After we are married, I can file on another 160 acres in your name and control another stream I know of. At my most recent count, I own 500 head of stock."

Louise turned to Claude and asked, "Mr. Stealer, how about you?"

Claude responded, "I control four water sources on a 160 acre homestead claim. I have over a thousand head of cattle, mostly longhorn from Texas. As soon as I send five hundred to market, I plan to expand a beautiful home that I am building on my land. Like Chris, I have access to thousands of acres of free-graze that belongs to the federal government."

Jon looked at Louise and could almost see her eyes clicking dollar signs as the auburn haired, hazel-eyed beauty smiled broadly at Claude. Before she could say, "I choose Claude," Chris defended his position. "Don't think that because he has a thousand head right now that his herd is better than mine. I shipped five hundred head last month before I sent you the passage money so that we would have money for our honeymoon. Besides, my herd has a number of the new eastern cattle mixed in. I don't have just all skinny longhorns; I am breeding them to new Charlet heifers. I should soon have heavier, higher priced beef to ship to market in the fall."

Louise was tempted by both offers, so she said, "When I have selected one of you, I will refund the passage money to the other. But, I would like ten days to make up my mind as to which one of you that I would prefer to marry. I would like to court both of you during that ten day period." Louise smiled her most flirtatious grin and sparkled her eyes at both men. Where the men saw stars, Jon saw dollar signs.

At the embarrassment of no men awaiting them and being left standing alone and unescorted by Jon, Sharon and Sonia felt resentment. Each of them stuck out their tongue at Jon's receding back. Out of the corner of their eyes, each noticed the others resentment and giggled together like two schoolgirls. They then proceeded together to the Harvey House Restaurant and entered by the side door and were seated on the opposite side from Jon and his cousins and their gentlemen friends. Being two very attractive young women in a town in short supply of the same, the Harvey House Restaurant manager immediately locked eyes on them and followed them to the table they selected, quickly taking a seat. He said, "If you two ladies are single and in need of employment here in Sante Fe, I would like to discuss with you about becoming Harvey House girls." After offering uniforms, housing and pay and many compliments about their beauty, he easily swayed the two ladies into accepting his offer. In fact, in both of their minds, they considered not becoming dependent on a man for their livelihood at this time a plus and quickly agreed to work at the restaurant for a while.

As Jon dined on the other side of the restaurant with his cousins and their men, Chris reached across the table in a boarding house grab for the grits and knocked over a glass of water in front of Louise. The front of her dress was doused with water. Louise thought, "Chris, you are no gentleman. In fact, you're rude and crude." She jumped back in horror. On her other side, Claude grabbed a cloth napkin and brushed the water from the front of her skirt, which if it had not been for her five petticoats underneath it, would have been a little bit too forward for Louise. Since six layers of material sheltered her and her mind was still rolling dollar signs, she accepted his courtesy. She said, "Thank you, Claude." Meanwhile, Chris turned red in his embarrassment. He knew that he had just messed up seriously and began apologizing. "Louise, I am so sorry that I knocked that glass of water on you. Please forgive me." Louise, thinking of Claude's better manners, more money and overall better looks, responded, "Chris, it will not be necessary for you to wait ten days for my answer. You were certainly rude grabbing that bowl of food like you did without so much as a 'Pardon me' and too, you are clumsy as well. I think that I would prefer to court Claude at this time."

In anger, Chris did not respond, but simply turned to Jon and said, "May I have my five hundred dollars back?" Jon reached into his money belt and grabbed out a wad of bills. He hurriedly counted out five hundred dollars in American greenbacks saying, "I am so sorry for the confusion that Louise caused. If you were rude by grabbing that bowl of food, she was equally rude by accepting money from two different men. I hereby apologize on behalf of Louise."

Jon stood and handed the five hundred dollars with his left hand and shook Chris's hand with his right. Then he asked, "No hard feelings?" Chris accepted the money, still beet red with his blushing and responded, "No problem, you probably saved me a lot of heartache. I certainly have been saved from a hard woman and I hope that Claude can put up with her." With that, he turned and left the room.

After enjoying their steaks, Jon talked about his work back in Holland. He had worked with a bronze bell factory that made church bells and shipped them all over the world. Therefore, Jon was familiar with the mixing of copper and tin to make bronze. He had helped install windmills around Rotterdam to pump the canal water back into the English Channel. These were very large windmills with wooden blades of forty-foot lengths. However, Jon had also worked on some smaller windmills further inland using the bronze blades technology. Mr. Steeler's ears perked up and he became more and more interested as Jon talked about his previous work on these windmills. He said to Jon, "I need some windmills on my ranch west of town. We can pump the water from the underground water table and provide more water for my stock. Would you be interested in taking on such a project, Jon?" Jon's eyes lit up and a smile came to his lips. "Sounds like a great opportunity and an exciting adventure. How much would you pay for such a well?" Claude responded, "We would have to see what the cost of the materials are, but tentatively, I would pay five hundred dollars plus materials for a well in the dry New Mexico ranch land I run my herds on. This would allow me to run more stock if I could get water to them." Louise, sitting at the table next to Claude, grinned with avarice in her eyes. Her mind was spinning with thoughts of more cattle, meaning more money.

Jon responded, "We could try the first well on that basis and renegotiate if the time involved was too extensive." Claude stood up, extended his hand and said, "Deal."

Still seated, Jon stuck out his hand and shook. Thus it was that Claude, Jon, and Louise departed the Harvey House Restaurant taking Mr. Steeler's carriage to his ranch.

In the subsequent days, Jon ordered the supplies that he needed and after riding over Claude's open range, selected a site near the railroad for the well. Jon commented, "Do you have anyone with a divining rod who can check this for underground water, Mr. Steeler? If we find enough water at this site, you likely could sell the excess to the railroad for their steam engines."

Claude responded, "You're right. What a good idea, Jon. There is an old Mexican lady near my ranch who uses a branch of a cottonwood tree to divine for water. Mark the spot with some rocks and I will have her come out and use her branch right here." The two men rode off on horseback in the cool of the evening in search of the Mexican lady. Arriving just as dusk was turning the sky pink in the west, Claude pulled his horse to a stop before a Mexican gentleman and asked, "Have you seen Teresa Montoya around?" The elderly gentleman said, "Si, senor. The second log cabin is hers," as he pointed northeast. Soon Claude had dismounted before the cabin and rapped on the door lightly. There was a response – "Who is there?"

Claude responded, "Claude Steeler, a gringo rancher looking for Teresa Montoya to do some divining for me. Is she home?"

"Si, senor," she said as she opened the door. "When do you want to start to look? If I am successful, the fee will be twenty dollars." She grinned and looked up at Claude with a twinkle in her eyes. Claude said, "If you find me some water, Teresa, I'll give you twenty five American dollars and a few Mexican pesos to buy your supper, too."

Teresa asked, "How far is it to you ranch, senor? Do you have a buggy?"

Claude turned to Jon and said, "Did you see that hostelry that we passed a few blocks back? Would you rent us a buggy there?" as he handed a number of old coins to Jon. Jon received the coins without comment and turned his horse toward the hostelry. Upon arrival, he dismounted from his buckskin, threw the reins over the hitching post and entered the stable. Jon spotted a small buggy in the center passageway and decides that would be fine. He approached the Mexican man on duty and asked, "Do you have a horse and buggy that I could rent in the morning, and if so, how much rent for a half a day?" Pedro responded, "Si senor. Twenty dollars American for a horse and buggy for half a day." Jon queried, "That seems a little steep. Is that the best you can do? Maybe you think that we want a big buggy, but that small one there would be fine. Surely that is not twenty dollars for half a day."

Several loafers were lounging on a bench near the hitching post where Jon's horse was hitched. They were favorably admiring his horse. One spoke up and said, "Pedro, this man entered town with Mr. Steeler. I'm sure that twenty dollars would not be a problem," he grinned mischievously. Jon relented and said, "I'll be back at daybreak to pick up the buggy if your stable would feed and curry my horse while I'm gone. That would be an agreeable price." The man grinned to himself thinking that he got the better end of the deal, but Jon grinned knowing that he had.

Jon returned to Claude at Teresa's cabin. He said to Claude, "The buggy and horse will be ready at daylight tomorrow. The price was twenty dollars. I hope that is acceptable." Claude responded, "It's pretty steep for half a day, but if we get water, it will be well worth the price. He rapped on the door again and said, "Teresa, I'll buy your breakfast at daylight in the morning. Be ready to leave then." From the rear of the cabin came a "Si, senor."

Later the next day, the three arrived by buggy at the pile of rocks by the railroad tracks. Jon stepped from the buggy and offered his hand to the elderly Teresa. He helped her from the buggy and then reached his hand back to the seat to grab the divining rod. She grasped the two ends of the stick between her hands and walked where Claude indicated. As she walked near the pile of rocks, the branch tipped down slightly. As she walked two or three more steps, it definitely pointed straight down. Old Teresa grinned broadly and said, "Senor Claude, you dig your well here where the branch is pointing."

Jon looks at her hands and saw that the bark had twisted from the branch where she held it tightly. The crumbled bark fell to the ground where she stood and Jon moved the pile of rocks to where the branch was pointing to mark the spot. He turned to Claude and said, "I will need to ship the supplies out here. And we will need some coal or wood to get a hot fire for melting the tin and the copper to make the bronze."

Claude responded excitedly, "When we get back to the ranch house, you make a list of what you will need and I will get my foreman started on transferring the materials to the site." Jon completed the list at supper and Claude's foreman put the materials on site that evening. Under the glow of the full moon, two of his vaqueros were left to guard the materials until Jon's arrival in the morning. In a few days, Jon had melted the tin and copper and combined the two in a pot, which was stirred with a wooden ladle producing bronze over the coal fire. This substance he transferred by bucket into a sand pit that he had dug in the shape of a windmill blade. Each blade was small; it stood only about eight feet. After each blade cooled in the sand for half a day, Jon flipped it out on the ground with a branch that he had trimmed for that purpose. After four days, these were attached to the well that he had been working on as they cooled. They had driven the pipes in the ground using mauls or sledgehammers. Water had begun to trickle from the pipe, indicating that they had hit water. With only thirty feet of pipe in the ground, water was already flowing from the underground water table. When Jon attached the blades to the windmill that he had assembled, the project was complete. He attached a bronze tube from the well to the pump and another from the pump to a galvanized tank bought for that purpose. He turned to Mr. Steeler and said, "Your windmill is working properly, sir. However, if you wish to sell water to the railroad, we will need to build a storage tank forty feet closer to the railroad in order for the engines to be filled. It will need to be built a few feet higher than the engines so that gravity can fill the tanks." Claude was so delighted by this prospect that before making a deal with the railroad, he sent his foreman to town to get the materials required for holding the tank above the level of the train's engine. He said, "Chip, pick up a large galvanized tank similar in size to this one we are watering the cattle with to hold the water for the steam engines." Chip responded, "Yes, sir," and turned his stallion for Sante Fe and left at a gallop, the stallion kicking up dust as he went. Within two days, that project was completed also. Jon designed a folding arm to transfer the water from the tank to the trains. Claude went to the train station and asked, "Who would I see about supplying water for your steam engines?" The ticket agent responded, "I'm in charge of this station. It would be my decision with approval from the home office in Denver. We always need water. How much would you charge to fill a five hundred gallon steam engine reservoir?" Claude grinned and said, "Depends on how thirsty your train is. We can negotiate the price later."

As the men returned to the ranch house, Claude said, "Jon, I am so pleased with all this and there will a bonus in it for you. I'll buy your supper and start you a small herd with five calves. You will need to register a brand. Jon said, "Can you show me how to do that?" Thus, it was accomplished that Jon registered the windmill brand in Sante Fe, New Mexico for his initial entry in the cattle business.

CHAPTER NINE

Some loafers had been watching from the stables as Jon registered his brand at the courthouse across the street. Two of them obviously were gun handy. Each of them had pistols in holsters tied down to their legs for fast draw. They grinned at one another as Jon returned for his horse, and one commented, "Hey, Dutchman! Are you the man who built that stupid looking windmill just down by the tracks?" Jon sensed the hostility and aggression in these men and simply said, "Si" and stepped into the leather and proceeded back to the Dutchman's Well. As they passed the ranch house, Claude, seated in a rocker, raised one hand and stopped Jon asking, "Jon, can I count on you to put more of those wells in strategic places around my range?" Jon responded, "Yes, sir, but the price is five hundred dollars and five calves for each one."

Claude said, "Deal" and stuck out his hand. Jon acknowledged and then continued on his way to the well. Before he could leave, Claude stopped him again and said, "Jon, in this country, it is best to go armed with at least a pistol. I see you have a rifle in your saddle boot. What model is it?" Jon replied, "Yes, sir, it's a Winchester 73. See the copper gleaming off of it? I'm a Mennonite and opposed to violence; however, if you feel that there is still an Indian threat in this area, I do have a revolver and holster. It's a Colt Navy 36, which I traded for in Charleston after receiving a forty-four from the Captain of the ship. Claude responded, "Better safe than sorry, Jon, but the thirty six caliber is a pretty small slug. Most of us out here carry a forty four for the extra knock down power and you would only have to carry one type of ammunition."

Jon pivoted in his saddle and reached in the saddlebag, pulling out his shoulder holster rig and Navy Colt and strapped it under his jacket and patted the spare cylinders for reassurance.

Jon gently touched his heels to the buckskin and was off in a gentle lope. The supply tent was still set up near the well. It was gleaming white in the noonday sun as Jon approached. He swung down and ground reined his gelding. Jon decided to unlimber his Winchester from the saddle boot. He took it in the tent with him and laid it across his folding cot. There he proceeded to clean it, while seated on the cot. Soon he heard the pounding of several horse hooves and lifted the tent flap with the back of his left hand and peered out. Approaching from the direction of Sante Fe were four horsemen. Jon recognized two of them as the two loafers from the hostelry in Sante Fe. They were accompanied by two more slovenly looking bearded men. Only their holsters and their guns looked clean; the rest of them looked filthy. The four of them pulled their horses to an abrupt stop in front of the tank. Jon laid his rifle on the cot and stepped out of the tent.

"May I help you gentlemen?" The nearest gun slick replied, "We overheard Mr. Steeler make a deal to sell water to the railway, but we are taking over instead. We will be selling the water and this will be our well now."

Jon responded, "Do you have any paperwork showing that Mr. Steeler has sold you this well," as Jon became tense, realizing the situation was bad. These were men who were obviously ready to use their guns to enforce their will, legal or not. Jon had his Navy Colt in his shoulder rig and touch it reassuringly. He remembered how easy he was able to center a shot in the middle of the skull and cross bones of the pirate flag during the Atlantic crossing, how the gun was just an extension of his right arm. He prayed, "Somebody is about to die here, Lord. I hope that you will forgive me for defending myself by using violence against violence. And Lord, I want to go to heaven, but just not today."

Jon watched the eyes and hands of each of the four men and decided in his quick appraisal that the most dangerous was not the speaker, but the one immediately to the left. His eyes were darting around and sweat was dripping off his brow. Jon knew that he would draw first. He continued to study the faces of all four and knew the best method of defense was going left to right in quick succession. When the speaker spoke again, he growled, "Step aside, Sonny, or you'll be hurt. It's four to one. You obviously don't know how this game is played." Jon did not respond but continued to appraise the four of them with his eyes. Jon stepped in front of the spinning and gleaming copper windmill blade reflecting the sun, which was beaming hotly overhead. The temperature was over one hundred degrees in the shade, but in direct sun, it felt like 120 degrees in the hot, dry, New Mexico climate.

Jon was cool and dry in the air, rapidly assessing his situation. The sun was reflected off of the blades into the four gunmen's eyes, as the blades continued to spin. Jon realized that firing left to right would give him an edge as the sun would hit them in the eyes one after the other. Jon slid slightly to his left because his body was blocking the sun in the speaker's eyes; so as he moved, the sun hit the speaker directly in the eyes. When he blinked, the man to the left of Jon, his eyes being settled down from the sun, drew for his gun. Jon beat him to the draw with his thirty-six caliber and hit him in the center of his forehead. The back of his head exploded in a spray of red as the gunman's bullet went off at his own feet. Jon began pivoting to his right immediately and moved left and shot again as the speaker drew his gun. Jon had moved left and the speaker's bullet missed him, but Jon's did not miss the speaker. A spray of red came from the back of his head as the shot slammed him backward to the ground. Jon continued to pivot right and dodge left; but the other two men, after seeing the blood spray from their companions heads, immediately turned and ran for their horses. Jon holstered his Navy, not wanting to kill unnecessarily. The Mennonite in Jon told him to let the men escape to a nearby cooley and the men disappeared.

Back in Sante Fe, the red tile roofs gleamed brightly in the sun and the sound of the gunfire reflected off of these red tile roofs. Claude Steeler and his foreman and the two accompanying cowboys all set out in the direction of the gun shots and to Dutchman's Well. As they approached, they noticed the two dead gunmen lying in two pools of blood at the edge of the well. Jon was nowhere in sight. Claude heard a retching sound from inside the tent. He proceeded to the tent flap and lifted it. What he saw was Jon with his head between his knees, spilling the contents of his stomach onto the sand floor of the tent. Claude said, "Are you alright, Jon? Have you been hit?"

Jon responded, "No, I was not hit, sir, but I still am violently ill knowing that I took two men's lives today."

Claude responded, "My foreman said that there are four sets of tracks heading to the well and only two leading to the cooley. I take it you faced four men? We may have to do this again, Jon, if two escaped. What led to the gun fight?" Jon said, "Their leader, the red headed one lying dead out there, told me that they were going to take this well away from us and sell water to the railroad. As the sun reflected in their eyes off the bronze fan blades of the windmill, I was able to take two of them out as they drew. The other two decided that it was too hot and left by way of the cooley. They suddenly decided collecting a bullet before they could collect the money from the railroad was too much of a price to pay and lost interest."

This day would later be known in western lore as "The Gun Fight at Dutchman's Well."

As ranchers in the area around Sante Fe learned of Jon's skills in building windmills and installing well pumps, he was frequently sent from range to range to hunt the elusive underground water in this dry section of the country. Steeler's ranch, which was mostly open range, was still inhabited by roving bands of Apache warriors. These red men were not happy with the intrusion of the white man into their hunting ground. The Apaches were one of the last tribes to surrender their independence and enter the reservations of the American government. They continued to escape across the Mexican border and were some of the best guerilla warriors that the world had ever known. They could hide behind a bush or rock and just fade into the background; you didn't even know they were there. The most successful general against them was General George Crook. He nearly had them under control now. One large band under the control of Geronimo was still at large, so a real danger of Indian attack still existed. Geronimo's band moved unencumbered across the line from Mexico to Arizona and New Mexico, particularly in the rough Rocky Mountain areas. This made Claude Steeler very concerned about the safety of his pending bride.

CHAPTER TEN

Claude decided to send 500 head of cattle to the sale barn in Fort Worth, to have enough money to complete the expansion of his house for his soon to be bride. He picked 6 of his best man to accompany the cattle to Fort Worth. Jon asked to go along to get away from the scene of the gunfight. Claude bought him a ticket to Fort Worth and asked Jon to look after his interest in the sale of his cattle at the Fort Worth Sales Barn.

As the train left the Sante Fe station, it rapidly accelerated to fifty miles per hour. Due to all the cattle cars, the train required two engines and a caboose.

Jon dozed with the click, click, click of the train wheels crossing the rails. By the time he awoke from his doze, they were approaching Amarillo, Texas. Jon felt relaxed in mind and body after he rested from the stressful gunfight at Dutchman's Well.

After passing just south of Amarillo, they reached the town of Canyon, Texas. The brakeman commented to Jon, "Three years ago, the last Indian battle of Texas took place in the canyon here." Jon asked, "How large is the canyon?" The brakeman replied, "Palo Doro is the second largest canyon in the United States and its territory. Only the Grand Canyon in Arizona is larger. Palo Doro runs for miles southeast of Amarillo and was the site of the final Texas Indian battle in 1874. You may wish to keep your eyes open as there are still a few renegade Indians." The brakeman continued, "If that's not enough headache, last year in 1876, we had a swarm of grasshoppers eating in a ten mile wide swath of every living plant, leather objects or house fabric of any kind, from Minnesota to Texas. We will pass that swath near Weatherford. You will notice even the trees were stripped bare. Each year, some new plants bud back out and the grass is returning. It was quite scary."

He continued, "I had a brother living in the path of that hoard of grasshoppers who lost all his leather harnesses, bridles, and other things from his barn, as well as the curtains from the windows of his house. Some people referred to these bugs as locust. I hope to never see that again," he concluded.

Jon noticed that the clicking of the rails indicated that the train had not slowed down for Weatherford, but just sped on towards Fort Worth. As the two engines began slowing, the coupling of the cars began bumping one against the other, to match the pace of the slowing engines. The cattle cars carrying the thousands of tons of livestock were hard to slow. In fact it took many miles to bring the train to a complete stop at the Fort Worth Livestock Pen.

Jon and the vaqueros began moving forward from the caboose to the horse car just ahead of the caboose to locate their horses. As the ramp was lowered, each vaquero placed a lead rope on the halter of his own mount and led him down the ramp to the ground level. Jon, with his horse Buck, was the last to exit the horse car. Once on the ground level, each man placed a bridle on his mount. Jon, too, removed the halter and eased the bridle over Buck's head, being careful of his ears. Jon had first warmed the bit under his arm before placing it in Buck's mouth. Jon dropped the reins to hold the horse still, while he tightened the cinch on the saddle. He stepped forward, patting Buck on the neck, speaking softly to him. As Buck was use to this procedure and not a horse to take a lot of air into his lungs, it was not necessary for Jon to strike him in the belly with his knee. Jon now stepped to the back of the saddle and proceeded to tighten the latigo, or back saddle strap, gently. This would hold the saddle in place in the event it was necessary for him to use a lariat cinched to his saddle horn.

Jon remembered that Sonia and Sharon had decided to go to work for the Harvey House Restaurant chain as Harvey girls. He knew if he ever returned to ranching near Sante Fe, he might see them at a Harvey House. Both were extremely attractive women, and with women being in short supply out west, Jon knew they would soon have marriage proposals. He wondered to himself, "Was he making a mistake by not ranching in New Mexico and finding himself a bride." But he soon forgot Sharon and Sonia when he noticed a young lady climbing up to the auctioneer's level above the auctioneer pen. Jon had first thought it was a cowboy hazing the cattle with a coiled lariat, slapping each rump in turn to move them into the sales arena. But when this 'cowboy' started climbing the ladder to the auctioneer's perch above the sales arena, he was quite sure it had to be a cowgirl, the way she was filling out those jeans. Next, she walked up to the auctioneer and handed him a note. She asked the auctioneer, "Would you read this note, please?"

The auctioneer nodded, 'Yes' and lifted the megaphone to his mouth and read, "Is John Roosma in the sales barn? If so, please raise your hand so this young lady may locate you." Startled by this announcement, Jon rose to his feet and waived his hat above his head. "Cherokee Nancy' noticed Jon right away and quickly dropped to the floor and proceeded to his location. As she approached his bench and promptly sat down next to him, she stared ahead at the sales arena and spoke out the corner of her mouth, "I have been looking for you ever since I heard your vaquero bragging about your well building for Mr. Steeler. The windmill pumps are a great idea, I believe. My Cherokee tribe needs a well at Comanche Ridge some twenty five miles south of here."

Startled, Jon eyed this dark eyed beauty and thought, "Cherokee? Comanche? Which is she? I know she is an Indian princess for sure, with that beauty."

He began putting his concerns into words. "You look some Indian, but you are more fair skinned than most. What is a Cherokee doing at Comanche Ridge?"

Nancy responded, "Well, I am lighter skinned because my mother was a white teacher to the Cherokee tribe when she met my father, a Cherokee carpenter. He is now working for General George Crook building Officer's quarters in Sante Fe, New Mexico. My mother Hazel has gone with him, but I am left behind alone. I am what people nastily call a 'half breed'. But, with my education from my mother, my Indian family shows me respect and looks to me for leadership. She continues, "Most of them call me 'Little Princess'," she blushed. She adds, "Some even call me 'Little Sure Shot' because of my skills with a rifle. However, since Annie Oakley has started using that name in William Hickock's Wild West

Shows, I don't like for them to call me that," blushing again.

Jon thought when she blushes red, she does look Indian, but when the blush is gone, she looks white. He said, "Well, I won't call you 'Little Sure Shot', but I will call you 'Little Princess' because of your beauty and grace." She blushed even more.

"You are certainly very kind with your comments, but I am here on serious business," she said. And as she turned to face him, her breast brushed his arm and Jon was immediately attracted to her. He thought, "How did I ever think this was a young man?" Then he said, "What did you want to ask me, Little Princess?" The Cherokee Princess said, "As I stated earlier, we need a well at Comanche Ridge. Our tribe is on one side of the ridge; the Comanche teepees are on the other side of the ridge, along with a stream for the local water. You see, as it is now, the Comanches are too aggressive and the Cherokees are too peaceful. Yet, we must pass by the Comanche encampment to get our water from the stream. It would be so much better if we had our own water supply on our side of the ridge. When I heard your cowboys bragging on the windmill out in New Mexico, I immediately wanted to get in touch with you to see if you could put a well in for the Cherokees at Comanche Ridge."

Jon thought, "Maybe I will go back to Sante Fe after building her a well here. Her mother and father are in the Sante Fe area. She may wish to go back there with me," he mused.

What he actually said was, "I love to build wells. That is what I did back at my home in Holland. As soon as Mr. Steeler's cattle are sold, I will be free to accompany you and do that for your tribe."

The Little Princess asked, "But can we afford you?"

"There will be no charge as I would welcome the chance to get better acquainted with you," Jon responded, looking her directly in the eyes.

"Oh, wonderful, I would love to get better acquainted with you, too," she said, grabbing him by his muscular arm with both her hands. She thought, "My, he has beautiful blue eyes."

And thus it was that the Cherokee Princess and the Dutchman well builder began their courtship at Comanche Ridge.

CHAPTER ELEVEN

Jon and Cherokee Nancy both rode their horses gracefully and rapidly arrived at Comanche Ridge. They were stared at in a hostile manner by some Comanche braves, which made them a little uncomfortable. As the braves lurked behind shrub brush in the area, both Jon and Nancy were aware of their presence. They both dismounted, keeping their horses between the Comanche and themselves. Cherokee Nancy quickly pulled her rifle from its case by the saddle and rested the fore stock on the saddle with the barrel pointing skyward. As Jon dismounted, he patted the two extra cylinders below his Navy Colt under his jacket. All of this was unobserved by the Comanche as their actions were hidden behind their horses. Nancy whispered to Jon, "I'll just step into the teepee with my rifle and watch your back until we know if they are hostile." "Great," responded Jon softly as he pulled the bridles from the two horses and hung them across the saddle horn, thus allowing the horses to graze with the other Cherokee horse herd.

While observing the Comanche braves out of the corner of his eye, Jon began searching for a suitable well site. Pulling his skinning knife from his left hip, Jon quickly slipped a cottonwood limb and rapidly trimmed it into a forked divining rod. Grasping the forked end of the cottonwood branch, he began walking back and forth on the Cherokee side of the ridge. Suddenly, the single end of the wishbone shaped device twisted violently downward, the bark grinding powder in his hands and the single end immediately pointing downward between his feet. Luckily, Jon then stooped to place a stone at the spot just as one of the Comanche braves loosed his arrow at this white intruder. As Jon felt the breeze created by this arrow as it passed by his head, he dropped flat on his stomach as he pulled his Navy Colt. As he pointed his Colt toward the Comanche, the day reverberated with a 'BLAM' of a gunshot. Jon's first thought was, 'have I been hit?' Then he realized that the rifle shot came from the teepee from behind him. Cherokee Nancy had proved herself a 'sure shot' as she downed the bow wielding brave. As there were three more braves in the nearby woods, Jon fanned his Navy Colt and emptied the five cartridges in the first cylinder immediately as he scattered shots in among the trees where the other braves were hiding. He quickly switched cylinders, placing a new loaded cylinder in his Colt and placing the empty one in the holster container. But there was no need for more pistol or rifle shots, as the Comanche braves faded behind the ridge as they slipped from tree to tree.

In the next few days, Jon had completed the well for the Cherokee tribe and over the evening campfire, he looked directly into the Cherokee Princess' eyes and asked, "Would you like to accompany me back to Sante Fe and visit your parents?" Cherokee Nancy just beamed, "Oh, my goodness, yes, that sounds wonderful. When can we leave?" Jon replied, "Well, my little bit of gear is already on my horse, so as soon as you are packed, we can leave immediately." And this they did.

Arriving back in Fort Worth on horseback, Jon purchased tickets for their train ride to Sante Fe. As Jon was picking up the tickets, the Cherokee Princess led their horses onto the horse car. She quickly stripped the bridles and saddles and dragged them down to the train platform where Jon joined her and grabbed the saddles up, one in each hand. Nancy was only a half step behind as they proceeded to the nearest passenger car. They were soon seated facing forward, with Jon on the aisle seat and Nancy near the window. At fifty miles per hour, they were soon back in Sante Fe.

Soon after their arrival in Sante Fe, Jon learned that all his cousins had married their husbands in his absence. He was delighted with this news and at the same time, was mildly disappointed that he had missed the ceremony.

CHAPTER TWELVE

Jon escorted the Cherokee Princess to the Cattleman's Hotel and got a room for her and one for himself. He asked, "Nancy, would you see that our mounts are placed in the stables behind the hotel while I carry our luggage and saddles to our rooms?" Just then, two bellmen approached Jon and offered to carry the loads for him. He graciously accepted their help and said, "Just place them by our rooms side by side."

As he then was free to step to the adjacent saloon off the lobby, Jon decided this would be a place to gather information. He stepped to the batwing doors and pushed them aside just as he saw Louise race her horse up the stairs hollering, "Claude, you better leave that wicked woman alone." Just then, the entire staircase collapsed, taking the horse and Louise to the saloon floor. Louise was thrown on her side amongst the broken timbers. Claude exited one of the cribs and peered over the railing at his wife lying in the rubble below. Jon was still trying to grasp exactly what had happened, but as there was no stairs any more for Claude to come down and help Louise, Jon went over and gently picked her up and held her until she regained her composure. Next, Jon grasped Louise's horse by its bridle and led the startled, limping horse out the street side batwing doors, where he looped the reins over the tie rail. Next, he gently ran his hands down the legs of the horse, feeling for injuries or breaks. Jon concluded that the horse was not seriously injured and went back inside to check on Louise. He decided that Louise was doing just fine also, as her mouth was loudly proclaiming, "Claude, our honeymoon is barely over and I am already catching you with another woman." She shouted to the top of her lungs. "There's gonna be hell to pay!" Claude then vaulted over the upper floor left from the broken staircase, and dropped the last three feet to the bottom floor to get to Louise. He started cooing, "Now, Louise dear, you've got this all wrong. One of my cousins works as a waitress here and I was merely visiting with her, so you just settle down, honey." He then put his powerful arm around her shoulder and led her out of the saloon. Jon was observing all this and he just smiled and thought, "Cousin, my eye!"

Jon then remembered that he had to soon meet with Claude about the cattle that he had been given as part of his pay for the four wells he had installed for him. He also had to pick up his two thousand dollars - five hundred dollars a well, plus five head of cattle for each well or twenty head of cattle. But with all the commotion, Jon felt this was not a good time as Claude had his hands full trying to settle Louise down. He then turned on his heel and went back into the hotel portion where he met Cherokee Nancy in the main lobby as she returned from putting their horses up.

Jon said, "Little Princess, let's go upstairs and place our luggage and horse gear in our respected rooms before we have a bite to eat in the Harvey House Restaurant. Later, after we eat, we can try to find your parents and let them know that you are here in town." Cherokee Nancy responded, "Oh, I'm not hungry; I couldn't eat a bite until I find my mother and father." As she was used to being very independent, she said, "Jon, you go ahead and eat while I look for them. I'll catch up with you later." And off she strolled in the direction of the fort. Jon agreed and crossed directly to the Harvey House Restaurant near the train track.

As he was seated, he glanced up and noticed Sharon waiting tables to the left, and approaching him from the right was Sonia. She asked, "May I help you, sir?" Suddenly recognizing him, she gasped and said, "Oh, hello Jon, what are you doing back in Sante Fe?" He responded, "Hello Sonia. It's good to see you." He couldn't help but notice how attractive she looked in her Harvey House uniform. "I have decided that I will start a ranch here in the Sante Fe area." He continued, "How do you like being a Harvey House girl, Sonia? Are you married yet?" She responded, "Oh, no, we can't be married and be a Harvey House girl. I did see in the Gazette where all your cousins are now married. How about you, Jon, are you married yet?"

Sharon observed Sonia with Jon and was immediately jealous. Suddenly, an olive skinned, high cheek boned lady, who reminded Sharon of Sonia in her facial structure and skin coloring, entered and without so much as a 'by your leave', sat herself down right next to Jon. This too infuriated Sharon. Jon glanced up and noticed the frown on Sharon's face and Sonia hot footing it back to the table with his drink. Jon, feeling crowded by the visual observation of three beautiful women, began blushing and diverted his eyes back to Cherokee Nancy and asked, "Did you locate your parents?"

Nancy smiled and reassured him that she had located them and said, "My Dad Thomas would like to meet you and wants to know where your ranch will be located." Jon said, "I look forward to meeting him, too, as well as your mother. As soon as I get myself settled in, we will have to get our horses and ride out and look for the ideal land for my ranch". And this they did in the coming weeks as their relationship continued to grow.

The End

I hope you have enjoyed "**Gunfight at Dutchman's Well**" and will look forward to further adventure of Jon Roosma in future books.

Dr. Carl R. Stekelenburg, LaGrange, Georgia, 30241.